FERGUS
the Highland Cow

Moo-velous Bedtime Stories

by
Tricia Purrier & Jen Stadler

Fergus the Highland Cow: Moo-velous Bedtime Stories
Copyright © 2025 Box Book Publishing, Tricia Purrier and Jen Stadler
All rights reserved.
This book, including the text, design, and layout, is the intellectual property of the author and publisher. No part of this book may be reproduced, distributed, or transmitted in any form or by any means without prior written permission from the publisher, except for brief quotations used in reviews or critical articles.
Portions of this book were generated with the assistance of AI technology, and edited, designed, and co-authored by Jen Stadler and Tricia Purrier.
ISBN: 979-8-9919015-4-3
Publisher: Box Book Publishing
boxbookpublishing.com

Table of Contents

Fergus Gets a Haircut ... 5

The Great Moo-sical Talent Show ... 9

Fergus and the Missing Mud Puddle ... 13

A Haggis in the Henhouse ... 17

Fergus and the Muffin Bandit ... 21

The Tractor Ride Disaster ... 25

Fergus Goes Camping (Sort Of) ... 29

Moo-velous Mud Day ... 33

The Day Fergus Thought He was a Chicken ... 37

Fergus and the Flying Underpants ... 41

The Bedtime Moo-sic Parade ... 45

Fergus and the Great Mud Pie Mishap ... 49

Fergus and the Giant Turnip Trouble ... 53

Fergus and the Midnight Moo ... 57

Fergus and the Very Mysterious Moo ... 61

Bonus Activities

Highland Cow Facts 65

What Would Fergus Do? 66

"I Spy" with Fergus the Cow 69

All about MY Fergus 71

Letters from Fergus 73

Bring Fergus Home 74

For every child who dreams big, laughs loud, and loves bedtime stories— and for the grown-ups who make snuggles and stories the best part of the day.

T. Purrier & J. Stadler
(and Fergus)

Fergus Gets a Haircut

Fergus the Highland Cow was very proud of his hair.

It was long.
It was fluffy.
And it flopped dramatically over one eye, which made him feel mysterious and important.

But today... the farm was hot. Really hot. It was so hot that Fergus's hair started to feel like a woolly oven on his head.

"I think it's time for a trim," said Granny McTavish, holding a pair of clippers.
"A TRIM?!" Fergus gasped.
"You mean a haircut?!"
He ran behind the barn and peeked out from behind a bale of hay.

Granny laughed. "Don't worry, Fergus. It'll just be a wee bit of a trim. Just a little off the top."

Fergus circled the barn while he thought about it.
What if he looked weird?

What if the ducks laughed at him?

What if his flop never flopped the same way again?

What if he looked like a "regular" cow?

Just then, Penny the Pig walked by with a flower crown on her head.
"You look cool," Fergus said.

Penny grinned. "It's hot out. You should try a summer style too!"

Fergus realized Penny was right. And he was so tired of being hot.

"Alright..." he said to Granny McTavish, "Just a tiny trim. And no weird stuff!"

When all the animals heard Fergus was getting a haircut, they all hurried to the barnyard to see.

Granny spun Fergus around to show off his fresh new do.

There was a tiny braid that kept his fur out of his eyes.
His brave, happy, kind eyes.
And yes... his flop still flopped.

"Fabulous!" said the ducks.

"Maaaa... I mean Moo-velous!" said the goat. And Fergus?

He gave a confident shake of his head, and his braid bounced in the breeze.

"Well," he said with a wink, "I guess I am a little cool now."

All of the animals agreed. And Fergus was glad he was brave enough to try something new.

FUN FACT FROM FERGUS

Highland cows have a special double-layer coat that keeps them warm in winter and cool in summer. But even Fergus likes a trim when it's toasty!

BEDTIME THOUGHTS

Even though Fergus was nervous, he decided to be brave. Has there been a time when you felt nervous about something? What can you do next time that happens?

The Great Moo-sical Talent Show

It all started when Millie the Chicken found an old banjo in the barn loft. She clucked excitedly, "I have an idea! Let's put on a talent show!"

Fergus perked up from his morning nap in the hay. "A talent show?" he asked. "Like… singing and dancing and stuff?" He felt nervous just thinking about it.

Millie nodded. "Exactly! Everyone on the farm can show off what they're good at!"

Fergus looked around. The ducks were waddling in rhythm. Penny the Pig was twirling in circles. Even the sheep were baa-ing in harmony.
Fergus suddenly felt even more nervous.

He didn't sing. He didn't dance. He didn't even know how to juggle hay bales (he tried once—it did not end well).

"What if I don't have a talent?" he mumbled as he watched the other animals get excited.

All day long, the animals practiced. Millie strummed the banjo and sang a country cluck tune. Penny prepared a ballet number called Swine Lake.

Even Granny McTavish agreed to judge the show and promised the winner a sparkly ribbon and an extra scoop of oats for dinner.

Fergus wandered off to think.
He mooed a little.
He spun in a circle.
He tried balancing a rake on his nose.
Nothing.

As the sun began to set, Fergus plodded back to the barn. His hair flopped extra low. "I guess I'll just watch," he sighed.

That night, the barn was twinkling with string lights. The hay bales were lined up like theater seats. The show was on!

Each animal performed their act. The crowd cheered, clapped, oinked, quacked, and baaa-ed. Then Granny McTavish announced, "And now... one last surprise!"

Everyone turned. Fergus froze.

"I don't have a talent!" he mooed.

Millie nudged him. "You don't have to perform. Just go on stage." So Fergus walked out. Slowly. Awkwardly.

And then something wonderful happened. All the animals started stomping their hooves and feet.
Thump-thump. Thump-thump.
It matched the beat of Fergus's slow walk.

Then Fergus did something he didn't even plan—he gave a big dramatic fur flip. His long, fluffy, fur swirled gently around and landed back on his head with a soft FLOP.

The crowd exploded. "MOO-VE OVER, EVERYONE!" yelled Penny. "WE'VE GOT OUR STAR!"

The next morning, Fergus woke up to find a sparkly ribbon tied to his stall. "Most Dramatic Entrance," it read. He grinned. Maybe I do have a talent after all," he said, flipping his fur one more time—just for flair.

Fergus realized that he didn't have to do anything extra to be special. He just had to be himself. That was special enough.

FUN FACT FROM FERGUS

Highland cows may not be known for their singing voices, but they do make low, gentle moos that sound like music in the hills of Scotland.

BEDTIME THOUGHTS

Fergus realized that it was enough to just be himself. All the animals loved Fergus, even though he couldn't do anything super special.

Even if you have something special you can DO, what is something you like about yourself, just because?

Fergus and the Missing Mud Puddle

Fergus LOVED his mud puddle.

It was the squishiest, slurpiest, most splatter-tastic puddle on the whole farm.

Every morning, right after breakfast, Fergus would do his famous SPLAT! right into it.

Then he'd roll and wiggle and flop until he looked like a giant, muddy meatball with horns.

But one morning, Fergus trotted out to his favorite puddle and—
"GONE?!" he gasped.

The puddle was missing! Only dry, cracked dirt stared back at him.

"Maybe it ran away," whispered Millie the Chicken, pecking at the empty spot.

"Maybe Granny McTavish filled it in," said Bailey the Sheep.

"Maybe," Penny the Pig added, "someone STOLE IT."

Fergus's eyes went wide. "A puddle thief?!"

He grabbed his detective hat (okay, it was a bucket, but close enough) and declared: "Let's solve the Mystery of the Missing Mud!"

The friends searched everywhere.
Behind the barn? Nope.
Under the tractor? Just a grumpy goose.

Inside Granny McTavish's laundry basket? Just some very clean, very soggy underwear.

Fergus flopped on the grass dramatically. "We'll NEVER find it."

Bailey looked up. "Um... Fergus?"

Dark clouds were rolling in. The wind was picking up.
A single drop of rain landed on Fergus's nose.
He blinked. Then he beamed. "I THINK IT'S COMING BACK!"

Rain began to pour, and puddles popped up everywhere—including right in Fergus's favorite spot.

His puddle returned with a glorious splash.

SPLAT!
Fergus rolled and squished and flopped like he'd never flopped before.

Penny laughed, "Mystery solved. The puddle just needed a refill!"

Millie added, "And don't go trying to hug me with that muddy fur."

Fergus grinned and Millie ran squawking away.

That night, Fergus dreamed of muddy splashes and rainy dances. Because sometimes, all a puddle needs is a little patience… and a whole lot of rain.

FUN FACT FROM FERGUS

Did you know cows enjoy cooling off in mud? It helps protect their skin and keeps bugs away. Mud puddles are nature's spa for cows like Fergus!

BEDTIME THOUGHTS

Sometimes it's easy to feel impatient when things aren't how you'd like them to be. Like Fergus, has there been a time when something wasn't how you wanted it and you felt impatient?

Next time that happens, can you try your best to wait patiently for it to get better?

A Haggis in the Henhouse?

One bright morning, Fergus was munching his breakfast oats when Millie the Chicken came squawking into the barn like her feathers were on fire.

"Emergency! Code Feathers! Intruder in the henhouse!" she shrieked.
Fergus blinked. "Intruder?"

Millie puffed up dramatically. "It's fuzzy. It's round. And it's growling! I think... I think it's a wild haggis!"

The barnyard went silent.

Everyone knew about the mysterious haggis. It was a Scottish legend—half furball, half grump, and completely bonkers. Penny the Pig once said they live underground, steal your socks, and only eat marmalade (that's jelly).

Fergus stood up tall (well, taller than usual). "Don't worry, Millie. This sounds like a job for... Detective Fergus!"

He trotted toward the henhouse, Bailey the Sheep trailing behind him with a magnifying glass balanced on her nose.

"I don't see any marmalade," Bailey whispered.

Fergus pushed open the door with his nose. "Shhh. We don't want to spook it."

Inside, feathers floated in the dusty sunbeams.

The hens were huddled in the corner, looking like feathered marshmallows. Then—a low growl.

Bailey gasped. "There! In the straw!"

Something fuzzy was definitely wiggling in the straw. Fergus gulped and stepped closer.

"Hello?" he said gently. "Are you a... ferocious haggis?" The growl turned into a sneeze. Then a tiny bleat.

Bailey blinked. "Wait a minute... that's not a haggis."

Out popped a wee baby lamb—curly-haired, sneezy, and definitely not a sock-stealer.

"Awwww," Fergus said, "It's a lost lamb!"

Millie squawked. "Well, it sounded like a haggis!"

Fergus gently nudged the lamb with his nose. "Come on, little one. Let's get you back to your mum."

As they walked out, the hens peeked from their corner, feathers fluffed and eyes wide.

"False alarm!" Fergus called cheerfully. "No wild haggis. Just one adorable lamb with a powerful sneeze."

Back in the barnyard, Bailey declared, "Case closed! Mystery solved!"
And Fergus added with a grin, "But let's keep the marmalade locked up… just in case."

FUN FACT FROM FERGUS

Did you know that human babies can't walk for about a year after they are born? But baby sheep, called lambs, can walk within a few minutes of being born?

BEDTIME THOUGHTS

The haggis in an imaginary creature that is not actually scary, because it isn't real. Let's invent an imaginary creature that is cute and friendly, and that would guard over you while you sleep at night.

What would its name be and what would it look like? What's something silly it would like to eat?

Fergus and the Muffin Bandit

The sun was barely peeking over the hills when a delicious smell drifted through the barnyard.

"Blueberry muffins!" Fergus mooed, trotting toward Granny McTavish's cottage with his nose in the air. "Fresh-baked and still warm!"

Granny McTavish always left a little treat out on the windowsill to cool. And Fergus always promised not to touch it. (And he almost always kept that promise. Almost.)

But today, something was terribly wrong.
The windowsill was empty.
No muffins.
Just some lonely crumbs... and a note!

Bailey trotted up behind Fergus, her wool in curlers. "What's going on? Where are the muffins?"

Fergus pointed with his nose. "Read the note!"

Bailey squinted. "'If you want your muffins back, follow the trail of crumbs. Signed... The Muffin Bandit.'"
They gasped.

"A muffin mystery!" Fergus declared. "To the trail!"

The first clue led them past the chicken coop. Millie was pecking suspiciously at something under her wing.

"Millie," Fergus asked. "Have you seen any blueberry muffins?"

Millie looked offended. "Do I look like I have muffins?"
Bailey peered at her feathers. "There's blueberry on your beak."

Millie huffed. "That's... from my breakfast jam."
Fergus sniffed the air. "Let's keep going."

Next, they passed by Penny the Pig, who was lounging in a mud puddle with a very full belly.
"Penny," Fergus said, "any idea where the muffins went?"
Penny burped. Politely. "Nope. Not me. Haven't eaten anything suspicious. Unless you count that button I accidentally swallowed."

Bailey looked doubtful. "A likely story..."
Fergus spotted more crumbs leading into the barn. "Quick, this way!"

They tiptoed into the barn, circled around a big stack of hay, and there he was! ... Jasper the Goat, fast asleep in the barn, surrounded by muffin crumbs, with blueberry on his chin. And one of Granny McTavish's napkins, torn to bits and stuck on his horn.

"Caught blueberry-hoofed!" Fergus cried.

Bailey tapped Jasper gently. "Jasper, did you take Granny McTavish's muffins?"

Jasper yawned. "Technically... I borrowed them. I was going to share. Eventually."
Fergus raised an eyebrow. "You left a ransom note!"
Jasper shrugged. "I thought it would make the muffins taste more... mysterious."

Just then, Granny McTavish poked her head into the barn. "Anyone seen my muffins?"
Fergus blurted, "We found them, Granny! They were... taking a nap with Jasper."
Granny sighed. "I was about to blame Farmer McTavish."

They all laughed, even Jasper—with crumbs still on his chin.

That afternoon, they baked a new batch together. This time, Fergus made sure to stand guard— because even on the coziest of farms... a muffin is never truly safe.

FUN FACT FROM FERGUS

Goats are known for being curious eaters, but they shouldn't eat muffins! (Especially not the paper wrappers.) Always feed animals the foods made just for them—even if they give you puppy eyes. Or goat eyes.

BEDTIME THOUGHTS

If you woke up in the morning and found that someone had taken your muffins and left a note, what would you do? Who would be the likely "Muffin Bandit" in your house?

The Tractor Ride Disaster

It was a bright and breezy morning on McTavish Farm, and Fergus had big plans.

"Today," he announced proudly, "I shall learn to drive the tractor!"

Bailey blinked. "Fergus... you don't even have thumbs."
"Details, details," Fergus said, marching toward the big red tractor parked by the barn. "If Granny McTavish can do it, how hard can it be?"

Bailey gave him a look. "Didn't you once get your head stuck in a watering can?"
"That was one time!" Fergus huffed.

Granny had gone into town, so the coast was clear. Fergus clambered up onto the tractor seat. It took him a while. He wiggled, shuffled, and got his fluffy backside stuck halfway. Bailey gave him a helpful push.

Once seated, Fergus grinned. "Now... what does this button do?"

Bailey squinted. "I think it starts the—"

VRRRROOOM!

The tractor roared to life. Fergus screamed. Bailey screamed. A chicken somewhere screamed.

And the tractor took off.

It didn't go straight.

It didn't go slow.

It went zooming in circles like a dizzy cow on roller skates.

"Fergus! Hit the brakes!" Bailey shouted, trotting alongside.

"I DON'T KNOW WHICH ONE IS THE BRAKE!"

Fergus's horns caught Granny's laundry line, dragging socks, bloomers, and a pair of her underwear behind him like a parade float.

Penny the Pig dove into a mud puddle for safety. Jasper the Goat leapt onto the roof. Millie the Chicken clucked a warning from atop the coop.

The whole farm was in chaos.

Fergus finally veered into the pumpkin patch, bouncing over vines and squash until... SPLOOSH!

The tractor rolled into the duck pond.

Bailey stood there staring, soaked from head to hoof.

Fergus sat on the tractor seat, wearing Granny McTavish's underwear on one horn and a sock on the other.
On the bright side," he said, "at least the tractor seat floats."

Bailey snorted. "You invented the first tractor canoe."
Granny arrived just as Fergus was wading to shore with a duck sitting on his head.

She stared. "Fergus. Why are you wearing my underwear?"
Fergus blushed through his orange fur.

Granny called Farmer McTavish to come help, and they towed the soggy tractor out of the pond. Granny McTavish patted Fergus on the head. "Next time, dear, maybe just stick to walking."

Fergus nodded, water dripping from his ears. "Agreed," said Fergus. "Though it WAS pretty exciting."
Bailey groaned.

FUN FACT FROM FERGUS

Cows are color blind and cannot see the color red. It just looks like a dull yellow to them. Cows are also really good swimmers.

BEDTIME THOUGHTS

Fergus had a thrilling adventure driving the tractor, but we should always let the grown ups drive. What is something you can't wait to drive when you grow up? What would be fun about it?

Fergus Goes Camping (Sort Of)

Fergus had been reading <u>The Brave Explorer's Guide to the Great Outdoors</u>, and now he had a mission.

"I'm going camping," he declared, proudly standing on top of a picnic table in the farmyard. He was wearing Granny McTavish's spaghetti strainer as a helmet and had a stick with a marshmallow tied to it like a flag.

Bailey blinked. "Camping? You hate sleeping outside."
"Correction," Fergus said, raising a hoof. "I hate bugs, itchy grass, weird owl noises, and mysterious night smells. But I love snacks, stories, and shouting 'BEAR!' for no reason. So I'm going."

Bailey sighed. "Where are you setting up camp?"

Fergus gestured dramatically. "Right here. Next to the chicken coop. Close enough to home for bathroom breaks, but far enough to call it an adventure."

Fergus spent the afternoon setting up "Camp Moo-squito."

He borrowed Farmer McTavish's shovel for a tent pole, used two quilts and an umbrella for shelter, and surrounded the area with pickles as "predator repellent."

"I read pickles confuse raccoons," Fergus whispered to Bailey, who didn't ask, but regretted standing so close.

That night, Fergus was READY.
He roasted a marshmallow (and half his eyebrow), told a scary story about a ghost cow who only moos on Tuesdays, and mooed a few campfire songs that made Millie stick her head in the hay.

Then came the sounds.
Hoooot.
Crrrick-crrick.
SNORT.

"What was that?!" Fergus yelped, clinging to Bailey like a fuzzy backpack.
"That was you, Fergus," Bailey muttered.
"I sound terrifying," Fergus said.

Just when Fergus began to relax, something rustled in the bushes.
"Did you hear that?" Fergus whispered.
Bailey nodded. "Yes. And no, it's not a bear."
"But what if it's a BEAR?!"

"It's the chickens, Fergus. They live here."

Still, Fergus climbed into the tent and pulled the quilt up to his nose. "Okay. Fine. I will sleep here, like a true adventurer." There was a pause.

"Bailey?"
"Yes?"
"Do adventurers get ice cream breaks?"
Bailey stared. "No."
Fergus sat up. "Then I'm going inside the barn."

Five minutes later, Fergus was curled up on a big pile of hay in the barn, safe inside a stall.

"Best camping trip ever," he said, to no one in particular.
Bailey shook his head. "You camped for twenty-seven minutes."

"Twenty-seven brave, snack-filled, mosquito-bitten minutes," Fergus corrected. "I deserve a patch."

FUN FACT FROM FERGUS

Did you know a cow can pee enough each day to fill 30 milk jugs? That's why Fergus wanted to be close to the bathroom (but we know real cows don't use a toilet).

BEDTIME THOUGHTS

If you went camping, like Fergus, what would you want to take with you? What do you think would be the most fun thing about camping?

Moo-velous Mud Day

It had rained for two whole days on McTavish Farm, and everything was sopping wet. Puddles filled the pasture. The ducks were delighted. Granny McTavish was not.

"Fergus!" she called out the window. "Stay outta that mud!"

Fergus, who was already halfway through building a mud slide down the hill, waved cheerfully. "Of course, Granny!"

Then he promptly slipped, slid, and did a full somersault into a puddle the size of a small pond.

McWhiskers the barn cat peeked from under a dry patch of hay. "You're going to get in trouble."

Fergus stood proudly, dripping with mud from nose to tail. "Correction: I'm going to start a mud festival."

Fergus called it Mud Day—a holiday he just invented that celebrated all things squishy, squelchy, and squishy-squelchy.

He made signs from old cardboard boxes:

Soon, the animals joined in. The pigs were all in, obviously. The chickens hesitated but got lured in by a worm tossing contest.

McWhiskers sat on a barrel with an umbrella and a clipboard. "Someone has to supervise," he muttered, judging the mud pie bake-off.

Fergus had games like:

- Slip 'n Moo: a very muddy obstacle course

- Mud Musical Squares: like musical chairs, but every square was a squelch

- And Name That Mud Blob: a mystery challenge involving Granny's garden gnomes and a whole lot of guesswork

Everything was going brilliantly until Fergus announced the grand finale: The Synchronized Moo-Slide.

"It's like synchronized swimming," Fergus explained, "but with more moo and less coordination."

They lined up on the hill, bellies down, and slid.
It. Was. Epic.

Unfortunately, the slide ended in Granny McTavish's flower bed. And even worse, Granny had just planted it yesterday.

She appeared with a broom and her "disappointed eyebrows," which Fergus swore could melt butter with a look.
"Mister Fergus Finneghan McTavish!" she bellowed.
"That's not even my name," Fergus whispered, shrinking behind a muddy sheep.

After some very splashy hosing down, and an apology bouquet made entirely from dandelions and one soggy daffodil, Fergus was forgiven.

Granny even admitted the mud pies looked almost good enough to eat. (Almost.)

That night, Fergus flopped into his hay bed, still a little damp and smelling faintly of swampy mud.
"Best. Holiday. Ever," he mumbled.

Bailey yawned. "Please don't invent any more holidays."
Fergus grinned in the dark. "Too late. I already started planning Feather Fest."
Bailey groaned.

Fergus drifted off to sleep, thinking about how the messiest days make the happiest memories.

FUN FACT FROM FERGUS

Playing in dirt and mud is actually good for you. It can make you happier, healthier, and helps you be creative.

BEDTIME THOUGHTS

Have you ever played in the mud? If you have a "Mud Day," what kinds of fun games would you plan?

The Day Fergus Thought He Was a Chicken

Fergus woke up one fine morning to the sound of clucking. Loud, panicked clucking.

He opened one eye and saw a flurry of feathers fly past his stall door.
Then another.

Then Millie clucked by, wearing a teacup as a helmet.

McWhiskers the barn cat appeared, munching on toast he had absolutely not stolen from Granny's kitchen.
"Morning," McWhiskers said. "Henhouse emergency."

Fergus leapt up. "Emergency?! Like—feathers on fire? Eggs exploding? A fox invasion?"

McWhiskers licked jam from his paw. "Worse. One of the chickens forgot how to be a chicken. The rest are losing their minds."

Fergus galloped straight to the henhouse, where a crowd of flustered chickens circled poor Clementine, the confused chicken in question.

She was sitting in a feed bucket, muttering to herself.
"I just… I don't feel like a chicken anymore. What if I'm not supposed to cluck? What if I'm supposed to MOO?!"

A hush fell over the coop.
All eyes turned to Fergus.
"I can help," he said, puffing out his chest. "I know a thing or two about identity crises. I once thought I was a rock."

"No you didn't," said McWhiskers.
"I stood very still for a full hour," Fergus insisted.
McWhiskers couldn't remember a time when Fergus was still for five minutes, except when he was asleep.

So, Fergus made a plan. He would switch places with Clementine. "She can find her true self," he explained, "and I'll step in as a temporary chicken."

No one argued. Honestly, the chickens were tired. And Millie couldn't wait to see Fergus as a chicken. So Fergus got to work.

He flapped his ears like wings. He made a nest out of laundry Granny had hung to dry. (She was not amused.)
He pecked at corn kernels—using his horns.
McWhiskers sighed. "This is undignified. Even for you."
Fergus clucked.

Millie blinked. "Actually... that was impressive."

Fergus wobbled around the yard, practicing his strut. He laid on a heat lamp (it was just a flashlight) and declared he was "almost ready to lay an egg." Millie the chicken rolled her eyes.

Meanwhile, Clementine was off taking a bubble bath and writing in her journal.

The next morning, Fergus attempted to crow like a rooster. It sounded more like a foghorn trying to yodel.

Granny opened the window and hollered, "If I hear one more 'cock-a-moodle-moo,' I'm putting you in time out—with the ducks!"
Fergus cleared his throat. "Understood, ma'am."

Clementine eventually returned to the henhouse, well-rested and back to her usual clucking self.
"I'm definitely a chicken," she declared. "I just needed a break."

Millie was so relieved. "Thank goodness," she squawked. "I need a break from Fergus being a chicken."
"Same," the other chickens clucked.

Fergus returned to being a cow, but not before leaving a little sign in the coop: "FERGUS THE CHICKEN - ON CALL."

McWhiskers glared at Fergus. "Just in case we ever have another chicken crisis?" he asked.

Fergus beamed. "Bawk bawk, buddy."

FUN FACT FROM FERGUS

Did you know cats aren't the only animals that purr? When a chicken is happy, cozy, and safe, they will close their eyes and purr softly.

BEDTIME THOUGHTS

What's an animal you would like to pretend to be? Let's hear you make its sound... but not TOO loud- it's bedtime.

Fergus and the Flying Underpants

It all started with laundry day.

Granny had strung three clotheslines between the barn, the apple tree, and the fencepost, and they were packed with freshly washed clothes flapping in the breeze.

Socks waved politely.
Shirts danced a little jig.
And somewhere near the middle—swinging like a banner of questionable glory—was a pair of Farmer McTavish's polka-dotted underpants.

They were enormous.
Like a parachute for a very stylish elephant.

Fergus wandered by, munching a carrot, and spotted them flapping like they were trying to take off.

"Those things could fly," he said.

McWhiskers, lounging on a hay bale, didn't even look up. "You say that every laundry day."

"But this time I mean it," Fergus said. "What if they do fly? What if Farmer's underpants get caught in the strong Scottish winds and end up in a different country- like America? What if they become American underwear?!"

McWhiskers blinked. "What is wrong with you?"

Right at that moment, a giant gust of wind whooshed through the yard.

It lifted a sock.
Then a tea towel.
Then—
WHOOSH!

The polka-dotted underpants launched off the line like they were heading to the moon.

Fergus gasped. "THEY'VE TAKEN FLIGHT!"

He galloped after them, yelling, "UNDERWEAR ON THE LOOSE!" McWhiskers, of course, followed—because someone had to supervise.

The underpants soared over the chicken coop, scaring Millie, three other hens and a rooster who, to this day, still has nightmares.

They bounced off the weather vane, glided across the garden, and snagged on Granny's scarecrow, who suddenly looked deeply embarrassed.

Fergus made a heroic leap and almost grabbed them—until the wind kicked up again and carried them up, up, up—
And then suddenly straight onto Fergus's horns.

"Are they on me?" Fergus asked, winded from the chase.
McWhiskers tried not to laugh. "Yes. Very much yes."

"I can't see them," he said, trying to glance sideways at his horn.
"You're wearing them backwards."
"I didn't know underwear had a front."
McWhiskers sighed. "It's the polka dots. They always point east."

Just then, Granny came around the corner with a laundry basket and froze. There, in the middle of the field, stood Fergus the Highland Cow... wearing Farmer's underwear on his horn like a very confused superhero.

Granny stared.
McWhiskers stared.
Fergus posed proudly. "I caught them."

Granny nodded slowly. "Well... at least they're not on the weather vane this time."
She plucked them off Fergus's horn and shook them out.

"They'll need another wash," said Granny.
McWhiskers wrinkled his nose. "So will my memory."

That night, Fergus lay in his stall, staring at the stars.
"Do you think underwear dream of flying?"
McWhiskers curled up beside him. "Only if they've met you."

FUN FACT FROM FERGUS

While it can get windy in Scotland, the windiest place on Earth is actually Antarctica.

BEDTIME THOUGHTS

Fergus wants you to use your imagination and think of something around the house that would be hilarious if it got lifted up and carried away on the wind. What would you do if that happened?

The Bedtime Moo-sic Parade

One night, just as the sun dipped below the hills of McTavish Farm, the animals settled down for bed.
Well—most of them.
Fergus was wide awake.

He had tried warm milk. He had tried counting sheep (which annoyed the actual sheep). He even tried reading a book titled 101 Ways to Sleep Like a Sloth.
Nothing worked.
And that's when Fergus had a brilliant idea.

"What if," he said, sitting straight up in the straw, "we had a bedtime parade... with music?"
Bailey the sheep opened one eye. "Why would a parade help anyone sleep?"

Fergus grinned. "Because it'll be a slow parade! A snoozy, cozy, dreamy-doozy kind of parade!"

He trotted out to the barnyard and banged a spoon on a feed bucket. "Attention sleepy farm animals! Tonight, we march... in the first ever Bedtime Moo-sic Parade!"

Everyone groaned.

"Some of us were ALREADY sleeping," grumbled McWhiskers.

"Put your pajamas on and meet at the apple tree," Fergus added. "Slippers optional!"

Five minutes later, a very sleepy (and slightly confused) group gathered at the tree.
Millie brought a tambourine.
The ducks wore tiny nightcaps.
Bailey brought a harmonica she didn't know how to play.
And Granny's cat, McWhiskers, brought a pillow and refused to march.

"Let's begin!" Fergus whispered (because it was a bedtime parade, after all).

He stepped forward, humming a soft lullaby:
🎵 "Moo moo moo, the stars are bright,
Time to snuggle in for the night…" 🎵

Millie shook her tambourine gently.
Bailey tooted something that sounded like a sneeze.
The pigs waddled along, swaying sleepily.
They paraded past the coop.

The chickens blinked and waved tiny wings before curling up again.

They passed the garden.

The tomatoes didn't care, but Fergus whispered goodnight anyway.

They circled the big oak tree, did a twirly bow, and marched right back to the barn—now even sleepier than before.

Fergus yawned. "That was the best bedtime parade ever."
Bailey flopped into the straw. "Let's never do it again."

The animals snuggled into their stalls, and soon the barn was filled with the sounds of gentle snores.
And Fergus?
Well, he finally drifted off—dreaming of marching bands made entirely of sheep in footie pajamas.

FUN FACT FROM FERGUS

Do you know the sleepiest animal? It's not the Highland Cow. It's actually koalas. Koalas can sleep up to 22 hours a day.

BEDTIME THOUGHTS

Did you know you can make up your own special bedtime song?

Go ahead, try it. It can be short and sweet... just sing about things that make you happy. Make it a habit to sing it every night before you fall asleep, and you'll have sweet dreams.

Fergus and the Great Mud Pie Mishap

One sunny morning, Fergus the Highland cow woke up with a rumble in his belly and a craving in his heart.

"I need a mud pie," he declared.

Millie the Chicken blinked. "A what?"
"A mud pie!" Fergus said, stomping happily. "Rich, chocolatey, gooey goodness!"

Penny the Pig snorted. "Uh… Fergus? A mud pie isn't actually pie. It's just mud."
Fergus blinked. "It is?"

Bailey the Sheep nodded. "Delicious to squish, not to dish."

But Fergus had already trotted off to make one anyway.

He squished mud.
He scooped mud.
He stirred in daisies for "flavor."
He even added a shiny rock on top. "A cherry!" he beamed.

The result?
A lumpy, gloopy, utterly inedible mess.

Just as he leaned in to take a big bite, Millie squawked, "Fergus, NO!"
SPLAT.

Mud on his face. Mud in his fur. Mud up his nose.

Penny couldn't stop laughing. "You're one of us now!" giggled all the pigs.

Bailey said, "Fergus, I think you need a bath."

Fergus sighed. "I was only trying to be fancy."

Millie fluffed his bangs with her wing. "You are fancy. But maybe you're not meant to be a baker."

They hosed him down with the garden sprayer, and Fergus giggled as the mud sloshed off his hooves.

Then Penny brought out an actual chocolate pie from Farmer Annie's windowsill.

Fergus took a bite and mooooed with delight.
"This pie is even better than mud!"
Millie nodded. "And way less messy."

"Maybe we should leave the pie baking to Granny McTavish," Bailey baa'd.

Fergus licked chocolate from his lips. He realized he wasn't that great at making pies. And he was okay with that.

FUN FACT FROM FERGUS

Cows have great senses of smell—up to six miles away! That's probably why Fergus started thinking about pies... he smelled Granny baking in her kitchen.

BEDTIME THOUGHTS

What kind of mud pies would you bake with Fergus? What would you put in your mud pie? Would you rather eat a mud pie, or a real pie? What kind of pie is your favorite?

Fergus and the Giant Turnip Trouble

One sunny afternoon on the farm, Fergus the Highland Cow heard giggles coming from the garden.

He peeked over the fence and saw Granny McTavish's prize vegetable patch—and right in the middle was the biggest turnip he had ever seen. It was surrounded by rabbits who were just staring and giggling because they couldn't believe it.

It was as round as a wheelbarrow and twice as muddy.
"Oh my shaggy fur," Fergus whispered. "That turnip is a gynormous!"

A sign nearby read:
"Do Not Touch! Turnip Contest Tomorrow!"
Fergus blinked.
Then blinked again.
Then very gently nudged the turnip with his nose.

It wiggled.
He giggled.

Just one little push, he thought.
So he pushed.
And the turnip rolled.
And it did not stop.

It bumped a watering can.
It bonked a wheelbarrow.
It knocked over three tomato cages and bounced off a row of rutabagas.
SPLAT!

The turnip finally stopped… when it splashed right into the the duck pond. And started to sink.

Fergus froze.
The ducks quacked.
The turnip bobbed.
Granny McTavish came running.

She saw the the top of the turnip bobbing in the water, just as it sank to the bottom of the pond. Fergus stood staring at it, wondering if he should have obeyed the sign.

"Oh, Fergus," she sighed. "You just can't help yourself, can you?"

Fergus gave her his very best I'm-sorry-but-I-was-curious face.

"Well," she said, tapping her chin, "I suppose we'll just have to enter a different vegetable at the fair."

She looked around the garden and spotted a big carrot peering out of the dirt. Fergus grabbed the green top and yanked it out proudly.

It was HUGE!
Granny grinned. "You know… there is a 'Carrot Contest' too."

The next day, the huge carrot won first place—and Fergus got a ribbon too… for "Most Helpful Garden Cow."

And from that day on, Fergus stuck to admiring the vegetables…
From a distance.
(Usually.)

FUN FACT FROM FERGUS

Not all carrots are orange. There are carrots that are red, purple, yellow, and white.

BEDTIME THOUGHTS

If you could have your own special contest, what would it be? "Biggest Watermelon?" "Stinkiest Sock?"

Fergus and the Midnight Moo

One quiet night on the farm, the stars twinkled like glitter in the sky and the moon hung low and sleepy.

All the animals were snuggled in for the night— except Fergus the Highland Cow.

Fergus couldn't sleep.

He had fluffed his hay.
He had turned three slow circles.
He even wandered over to the barn door and had even tried counting sheep (but even the sheep were sleeping, so no one was jumping the fence).

Nothing worked. Fergus was still wide awake.
So, he gave a soft little "moo," just in case someone else was awake.

Nothing.

He tried a slightly louder "Moo?"
Still no answer.

Finally, Fergus gave a big "MOOOOO" that echoed all the way to the barn roof.

Suddenly, a window creaked open and Millie the chicken popped her head out. She was grumpy.
"Some of us are trying to sleep, you know!"

"Sorry," Fergus whispered. "I was just... lonely."

Millie clucked, "Try counting clouds."

Fergus looked up. The clouds looked like sheep. He saw one that looked like Bailey with a hat on her head. He started to giggle... which only made him more awake.

So he tiptoed (as best a cow can tiptoe) over to the pond. There, he saw a sleepy duck floating like a little boat.

"Can't sleep," Fergus whispered.

The duck yawned. "Try humming a lullaby."

Fergus tried. It sounded more like a low, wobbly trumpet.
"Okay, maybe not," quacked the duck as he paddled away.

Just when Fergus thought he'd be up until sunrise, a soft voice said, "Can't sleep either?"

It was Molly, the tiny barn kitten, with her tail curled up like a pillow.

Fergus nodded. "I've tried counting and humming and mooing and tiptoeing."

Molly stretched and said, "Sometimes it helps just to be still and quiet… with a friend."

So Fergus lay down in the grass, and Molly curled up on his back. Together, they listened to the night sounds—
the crickets, the rustle of leaves, the soft hoot of an owl.

Fergus gave one last little "Moo…"
But this time, it was the sleepy kind.
And before long,
both Fergus and Molly
were snoring gently
under the stars.

FUN FACT FROM FERGUS

Did you know that having the same bedtime routine every night before bed will eventually train your brain that it's time to go to sleep?

BEDTIME THOUGHTS

What are some things you can do every night before bed that will start to help you fall asleep? It could turning the lights down, putting on pjs, brushing teeth, reading a story, and snuggling with your favorite stuffy. What will you do?

Fergus and the Very Mysterious Moo

It started with a moo.

But not a normal Fergus kind of moo.
This one was high-pitched.

And squeaky.
And came from the henhouse.

Fergus froze mid-chew on a mouthful of hay.
He looked toward the hens.
"Did… did one of you just moo?" he asked.

The hens stared back, wide-eyed.
"We lay eggs, Fergus," clucked one. "We do not moo."

Another loud SQUEAKY MOO! echoed across the farm.

Fergus's eyes got big. "There it is again!"

So he trotted over to the pigpen.
"Any of you mooing today?"

The pigs just snorted. "Try the goats."

Fergus clomped over to the goat pen.
The goats were standing on their house (as usual), nibbling on a garden glove.

"We've never mooed a day in our lives," said Jasper the goat. "Sounds like you've got a ghost cow!"

Fergus gasped. "A ghost cow?!"
Jasper nodded solemnly. "Yup. Probably looking for snacks."
"Sn-snacks?" Fergus squeaked.
"Or maybe a nap," said another goat. "I'd love a nap myself."

Fergus mooooed so loudly in fright, he startled himself.

Then— just as he was tip-hoofing toward the barn to hide— the squeaky moo rang out again.

But this time... it was followed by a giggle.

Fergus turned slowly.

Out popped Molly the barn kitten, wearing an upside-down yogurt cup on her head.

"I made a megamoo machine!" she said proudly. "You talk into the cup, and it makes your voice sound funny!"

She gave another high-pitched moo into the cup.
It echoed off the barn and made the ducks dive into the pond.

Fergus blinked.
Then... laughed so hard he nearly fell over.

"I thought there was a haunted cow!" he said between snorts.

"Nope," said Molly. "But if you ever need me to help roundup the herd, I think I can do it," she meowed proudly.

Fergus winked. "You make a VERY convincing cow," he mooed back.

FUN FACT FROM FERGUS

While everyone knows cows "moo," there are also other animals that can make sounds that can be mistaken for a cow's moo. Some of these include elk, giraffes, spotted hyenas, and certain birds like the Capuchinbird.

BEDTIME THOUGHTS

Let's hear your best "moo." Can you also "meow" like Molly? What other animal sounds can you make? How do you think Fergus would moo "goodnight"?

Highland Cow Facts
(From the Highlands to your Heart)

- Fergus is a Highland Cow (also called a "coo" in Scotland)! These cows are famous for their long, shaggy hair and sweet temperaments.

- Their thick coat keeps them warm during chilly Highland winters—and yes, it grows right over their eyes!

- Highland cows are one of the oldest cattle breeds in the world and have been around for hundreds of years.

- They love to graze, nap, and get scratches behind their ears (just like Fergus).

- In real life, Highland cows come in many colors: red, black, yellow, brindle, and even white!

- Fergus may be extra silly, but Highland cows really are known for their calm and friendly nature.

What Would Fergus Do?

Fergus the Highland Cow is always getting into funny, messy, and sometimes sticky situations on the farm. Here, you'll read about a few of the curious things that happen to Fergus and his friends.

Your job? Use your imagination! Think about what you think Fergus would do. Picture it in your mind. Maybe he sings a song, or builds something out of hay bales, or gives someone a big, fluffy hug.

There are no wrong answers—just good, kind, and silly ideas!

You can always come back and try to think of new and creative ways to help Fergus in these situations.

Have even more fun by taking some paper and crayons and drawing a picture of these little story ideas.

1. Fergus sees a lonely chicken sitting all by herself at snack time. What would Fergus do to cheer her up?

2. It starts raining and Fergus forgot his umbrella... again. What clever thing would Fergus do to stay dry?

3. Jasper the goat is stuck on the roof (again). How would Fergus try to help him get down?

4. Fergus finds a mysterious, muddy boot in the middle of the garden. What would he do with it?

5. Bailey the sheep is nervous about dancing at the farm talent show. What would Fergus say or do to help her feel brave?

6. Granny McTavish accidentally dropped her sandwich in the mud. How could Fergus try to fix the lunchtime disaster?

7. Fergus wants to surprise his friends with something special. What kind of surprise would he plan?

8. The wind blows Fergus's bedtime blanket out of the barn. Where would he go to find it—and who might help?

9. Fergus hears a strange noise coming from the vegetable patch at night. What does he do to investigate?

10. One of Fergus's friends is having a very grumpy day. What silly thing might Fergus do to make them laugh?

11. Fergus sees a baby duckling trying to reach the top of a haystack. What would he do?

12. There's only one cookie left on the plate... and Fergus and Molly the kitten both want it. What would Fergus do?

13. Fergus wants to give Granny McTavish a gift to say thank you. What would he make or find?

14. A visitor comes to the farm who's never met a Highland cow before. What does Fergus do to welcome them?

15. Fergus didn't listen and did something Granny McTavish told him not to do. What will he do next?

Thank you for helping Fergus figure out how to solve these problems. You're a GREAT friend!

I Spy With Fergus the Highland Cow

Fergus loves to spy interesting things all around him—on the farm, in the garden, and even in his dreams!

Can you be a curious cow too?

Use your eyes, your imagination, and maybe a little giggle power to find things that match these clues.

You can play indoors, outdoors, or just in your mind!

This list can be used over and over again. Can you spy different things each time?

Fergus Says, "I Spy..."

- Something that starts with the same letter as your name
- Something that is fuzzy, fluffy, or frizzy
- Something that makes a funny noise
- Something that is smaller than a turnip
- Something that smells sweet (or a little stinky!)
- Something that could be a blanket for a chicken
- Something that you think Fergus would try to eat
- Something that could be used as a hat in an emergency
- Something that is round like a cow pie (Ew! But true!)
- Something that would make Bailey the sheep laugh
- Something that could be part of a silly invention
- Something that might hide a squirrel
- Something that could be used in a goat juggling contest
- Something that Fergus would say is his favorite color
- Something that is too big to fit in your sock drawer
- Something that makes you smile just looking at it

All About My Fergus!

Fergus the Highland Cow is one-of-a-kind... just like you!

This is where you get to imagine your own version of Fergus.
What does he love?
What makes him laugh?
What kind of silly things might he do on your farm?

Fill in the blanks to create a Fergus that's just right for you.

Name: _____

(Maybe you want to keep him Fergus... or give him a middle name like "Pickles"!)

Favorite Food: _____

(Spoiler alert: he loves turnips, but maybe yours prefers pizza?)

Favorite Color: _____

Best Friend's Name: _____

(Could be a goat, a duck, or even a dragon!)

What makes him laugh: _____

Fergus is afraid of: _____

(Sometimes big cows have big feelings too!)

If Fergus had a job, he would be a: _____

(Firefighter? Dance teacher? Royal cheese taster?)

Fergus's silliest habit: _____

(Maybe he sings to potatoes? Who knows!)

Fergus's favorite bedtime story: _____

One word to describe your Fergus: _____

LETTERS FROM FERGUS

If you enjoyed reading stories about Fergus, you'll LOVE receiving personal letters from him each week!!

Sign up for "The Fergus Adventure," and receive a weekly email or letter from Fergus for six weeks. Fergus will send you an email (or a letter) from the farm in Scotland, telling you all about his daily adventures. He'll also send you more "Fun Facts," trivia, activities, challenges, and coloring pages.

Scan the QR Code below, or visit boxbookpublishing.com to learn more or to sign up for this FREE Fergus Adventure!

THANK YOU

Thank you for purchasing Moo-velous Bedtime Stories! At Box Book Publishing, we want families to make the most of their memories together!

If you enjoyed this book, please consider taking a moment to leave us a review on Amazon. It helps us spread goodness!

BRING FERGUS HOME!

Do you wish you could snuggle Fergus right before bedtime?

Well... guess what? Fergus found a cuddly twin that looks just like him—soft, fuzzy, and ready for adventures (or naps)!

If you'd like to see Fergus's fluffy friend, just scan the QR code below and visit our website. Information about this lovable stuffed Highland Cow is on our Fergus Adventure page!

Printed in Dunstable, United Kingdom